Clown Painting His House

Written by Jill Eggleton
Illustrated by Stella Yang

Rigby

Clown looked
at his house.

"My house is old,"
said Clown.

"I will paint it
today."

Clown made a list.

paint

ladder

brush

He looked
in the shed.

"I have paint.
I have a ladder.
I have no brush,"
said Clown.

Clown saw
a big broom.

"A broom,"
said Clown.

"Good! I will
paint my house
with this."

Clown painted
the roof.

He painted
the roof blue.

"The roof
looks good,"
said Clown.

Clown painted
the doors.

He painted
the doors green.

"The doors
look good,"
said Clown.

Yes, yes, yes.

Clown painted
the walls.

He painted
the walls yellow.

Clown looked
at his house.

He looked
and looked
and looked.

"Help!" said Clown.
"Where are the windows?"

A Shopping List

Guide Notes

Title: Clown Paints His House
Stage: Early (2) – Yellow

Genre: Fiction
Approach: Guided Reading
Processes: Thinking Critically, Exploring Language, Processing Information
Written and Visual Focus: List, Speech Bubbles
Word Count: 129

THINKING CRITICALLY
(sample questions)
• What do you think this story could be about?
• Focus on the title and discuss.
• Why did Clown use a broom to paint his house?
• Why do you think Clown painted over the windows?
• What do you think Clown will do now that he has painted his windows?

EXPLORING LANGUAGE

Terminology
Title, cover, illustrations, author, illustrator

Vocabulary
Interest words: paint, ladder, brush, shed, broom, roof, doors, walls, windows
High-frequency words (reinforced): his, made, saw, good, with, looks
Positional word: in

Print Conventions
Capital letter for sentence beginnings and names (**C**lown), periods, quotation marks, commas, exclamation marks, question mark